MAR 0 6

Mural on Second Avenue

To Kim Casper, who understands friendship
L. M.

I dedicate this book to my Mom, my Grandma, and to the artist who
spent endless days and nights painting the Mural on Second Avenue.
R. K.

"City Moon" copyright © 2005 by Lilian Moore
"¡Hola, niño!" from *I Never Did That Before* copyright © 1995 by Lilian Moore
"Mural on Second Avenue" from *Something New Begins* copyright © 1982 by Lilian Moore
"In the Park" from *Think of Shadows* copyright © 1980 by Lilian Moore
"The Bridge," "Construction," "Forsythia Bush," "Pigeons," "Rain Pools," "Reflections," "Roofscape,"
"Snowy Morning," "Summer Rain," "To a Red Kite," "The Tree on the Corner," and "Winter Dark"
from *I Thought I Heard the City* copyright © 1971 by Lilian Moore
"How to Go Around a Corner" from *I Feel the Same Way* copyright © 1967 by Lilian Moore
Illustrations copyright © 2005 by Roma Karas

First edition 2005

Library of Congress Cataloging-in-Publication Data

Moore, Lilian.
Mural on Second Avenue, and other city poems / Lilian Moore ; illustrated by Roma Karas. — 1st ed.
p. cm.
Summary: A collection of poems that capture various aspects of life in the city.
ISBN 0-7636-1987-6
1. Cities and towns —Juvenile poetry. 2. City and town life—Juvenile poetry. 3. Children's poetry,
American. [1. City and town life—Poetry. 2. American poetry.] I. Karas, Roma, ill. II. Title.
PS3563.O622 M66 2004
811'.54 — dc21   2002073702

2 4 6 8 10 9 7 5 3 1

Printed in China

This book was typeset in Badger.
The illustrations were done in oil.

Candlewick Press
2067 Massachusetts Avenue
Cambridge, Massachusetts 02140

visit us at www.candlewick.com

Mural on Second Avenue
and Other City Poems

Lilian Moore
illustrated by Roma Karas

CANDLEWICK PRESS
CAMBRIDGE, MASSACHUSETTS

Snowy Morning

Wake
gently this morning
to a different day.
Listen.

There is no bray
of buses.
No brake growls,
no siren howls, and
no horns
blow.

There is only
the silence
of a city
hushed
by snow.

Winter Dark

Winter dark comes early
mixing afternoon
and night.
Soon
there's a comma of a moon,

and each streetlight
along the
way
puts its period
to the end of day.

Now
a neon sign
punctuates the dark
with a bright
blinking
breathless
exclamation mark!

Roofscape

The lines are
straight
and
many-cornered —
plunging,
rising high.

From my window
I can see
how roofs
design a sky.

How to Go Around a Corner

Corners
are
the places
where
streets run down to meet.

Corners
are
surprises
on almost any street.

At
almost
any corner
it's best to wait

and
turn
the corner
slowly
as if it had a gate.

¡Hola, niño!

"¡Hola, niño!"
Mr. Santos greets me
when he meets me
in the street.

I never knew
what to say
before.

Now when he calls
"¡Hola, niño!"
I say "¡Hola, señor!"

¡Hola, niño! (OH-la NEEN-yo): Hello, little boy!
¡Hola, señor! (OH-la sen-YOR): Hello, sir!

Reflections

On this street
of windowed stores,
see
in the glass
shadow people meet
and pass
and glide to
secret places.

Ghostly mothers
hold
the hands of dim gray
  children,
scold
them silently
and melt away.

And
now and then,
before
the window mirror
of a store,
phantom faces
stop
and window shop.

To a Red Kite

Fling
yourself
upon the sky.

Take the string
you need.
Ride high

high
above the park.
Tug and buck
and lark
with the wind.

Touch a cloud,
red kite.
Follow the wild geese
in their flight.

Forsythia Bush

There is nothing
quite
like the sudden
light

of
forsythia
that
one morning
without warning

explodes
into yellow
and
startles the street
into spring.

In the Park

When you've
run races
in the sun,

stolen bases,
pumped high on a
swing,

when you've
jumped Double Dutch
too much,

played

till you're sun drunk
sun dizzy —

how shivery cool
to fling
yourself
into the tree's great
pool
of
shade.

Rain Pools

The rain
litters
the street
with mirror splinters,
silver,
brown.

Now
each piece
glitters with

sky
cloud
tree

upside down.

Summer Rain

The sky is
scrubbed
of every smudge of
cloud.

The sidewalk is a
slate
that's quickly
dry.

Light
dazzles
like
a washed
windowpane,

and

I

breathe
the freshly laundered
air
of after-rain.

Construction

The giant mouth
chews
rocks
spews them
and is back for
more.

The giant arm
swings up
with a girder
for
the fourteenth floor.

Down there,
a tiny man
is
telling them
where
to put a skyscraper.

Pigeons

Pigeons are city folk
content
to live with concrete
and cement.

They seldom
try
the sky.

A pigeon never sings
of hill
and flowering hedge
but busily commutes
from sidewalk
to his ledge.

Oh, pigeon, what a waste of wings!

The Tree on the Corner

I've seen
the tree on the corner
in spring bud
and summer green.
Yesterday
it was yellow gold.

Then a cold
wind began to blow.
Now I know —
you really do not see
a tree
until you see
its bones.

Mural on Second Avenue

Someone
stood here
tall on a ladder,
dreaming
to the slap of a
wet brush,

painting
on the blank
unwindowed wall of
this old house.

Now the wall is a
field of wild
grass,
bending to a wind.

A unicorn's grazing there
beside a
zebra.

A giraffe
is nibbling a
treetop

and in a sky of
eye-blinking
blue

a horse is flying.

All
right at home in the
neighborhood.

The Bridge

A bridge
by day
is steel and strong.
It carries
giant trucks that roll along
above the waters
of the bay.
A bridge is steel and might —
till night.

A bridge
at night
is spun of light
that someone tossed
across the bay
and someone caught
and pinned down tight —
till day.

City Moon

Above the neon
glare, where words
flash and dance,

above the glowing
windows of tall
buildings,

above the runway
lights that call to
planes

rushing like
comets through
the
night sky,

a pale moon rises
and hopes to be
noticed.

Index of First Lines